Look Closer!

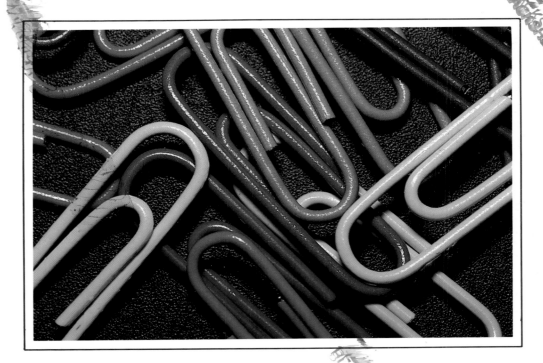

Peter Ziebel

Clarion Books

New York

ACKNOWLEDGMENTS

The author wishes to thank the families of the children who posed for some of the photographs in this book: the Andersons, the Clementses, the Dillons, the Krists, the Mosbachers, the Rosens, and the Whites. He is also grateful for the advice and encouragement from many friends, especially Bob Krist and Wendel White, and for the patience and support (in many forms) provided by the Parental and In-Law Foundation.

Clarion Books
a Houghton Mifflin Company imprint
52 Vanderbilt Avenue, New York, NY 10017
Text and photographs copyright © 1989 by Peter Ziebel

Library of Congress Cataloging-in-Publication Data
Ziebel, Peter.
Look closer! / by Peter Ziebel.
p.   cm.
Summary: Close-up photographs present unusual views of common items, such as a toothbrush, orange, or umbrella, accompanied by brief questions providing a clue to each object's identity.
ISBN 0-89919-815-5
[1. Visual perception.]   I. Title.
PZ7.Z485Lo   1989   88-29186
[E]—dc19   CIP
AC

H   10 9 8 7 6 5 4 3 2 1

For my wife, Edie

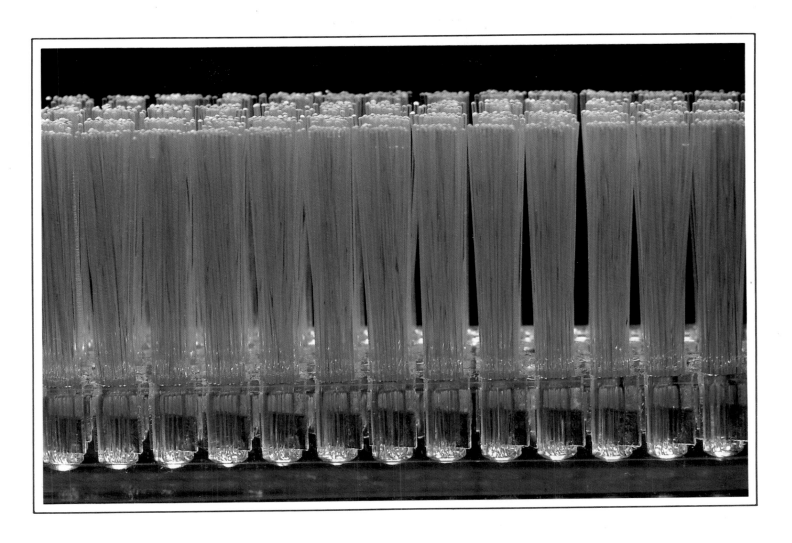

What keeps your teeth clean?

A toothbrush

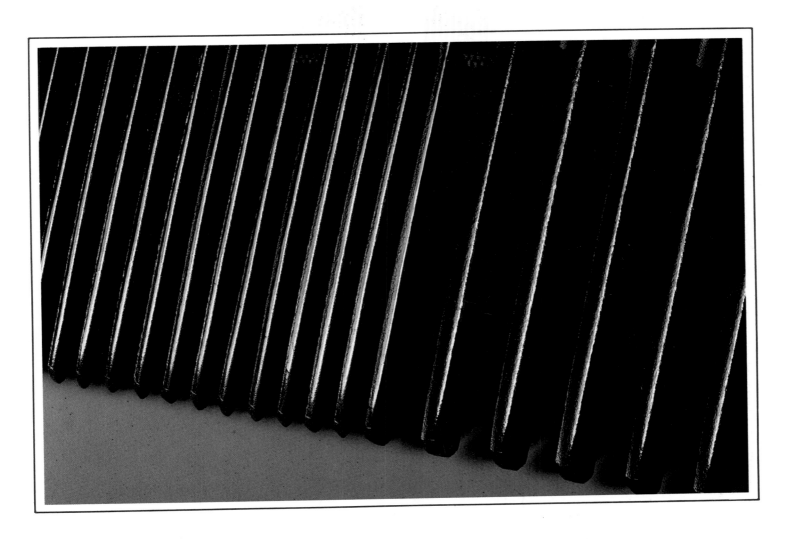

What untangles your hair?

A comb

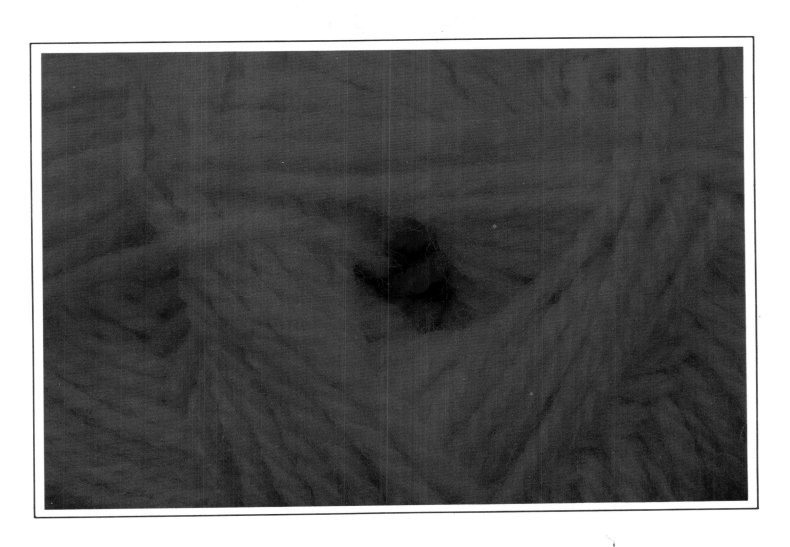

What do you use to knit?

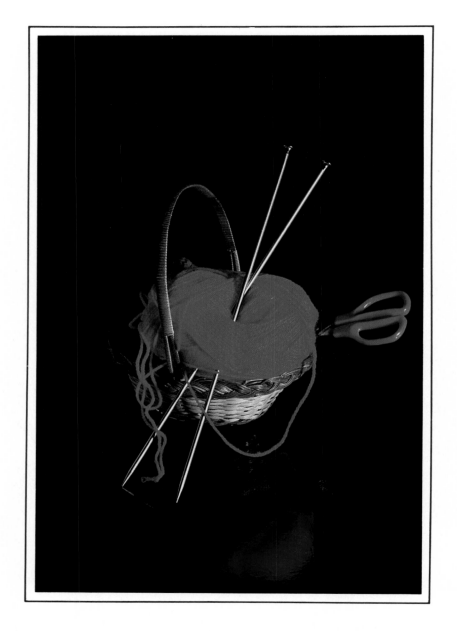

A ball of yarn

What do you wear to feel warm?

A sweater

What is a warm and furry friend?

A cat

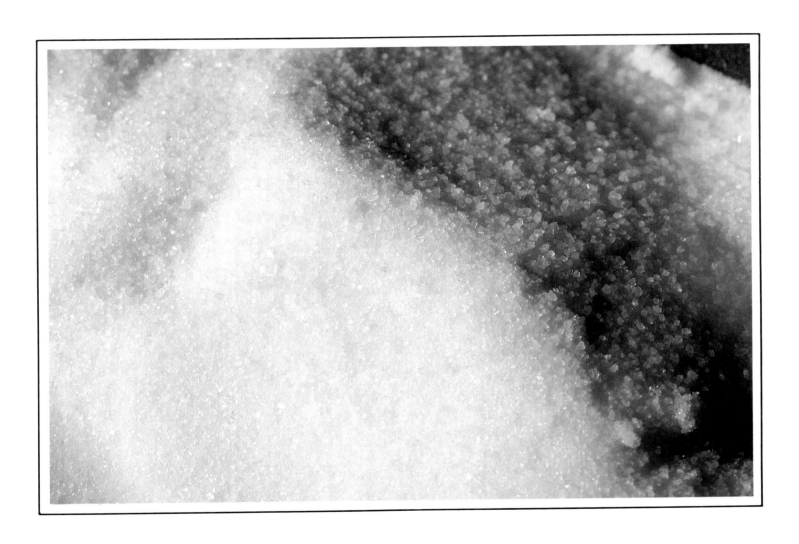

What tastes sweet?

Sugar

What is juicy?

An orange

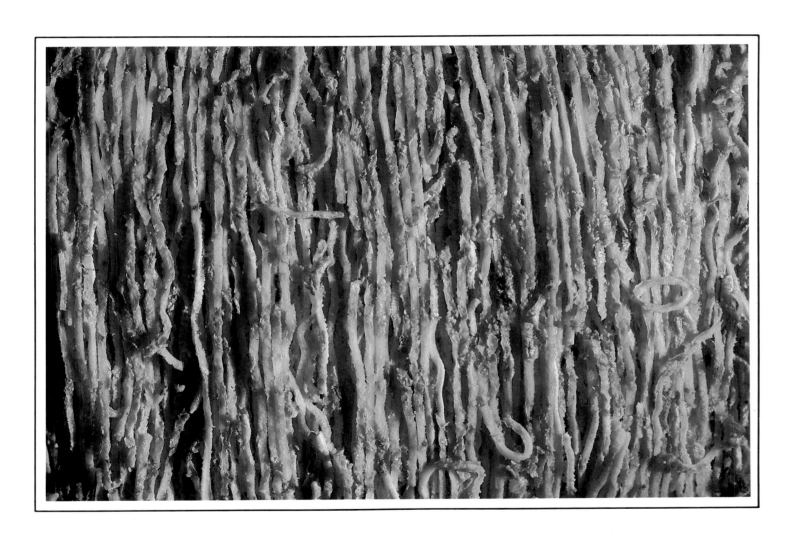

What can you eat for breakfast?

Shredded wheat

What keeps you dry in the rain?

An umbrella

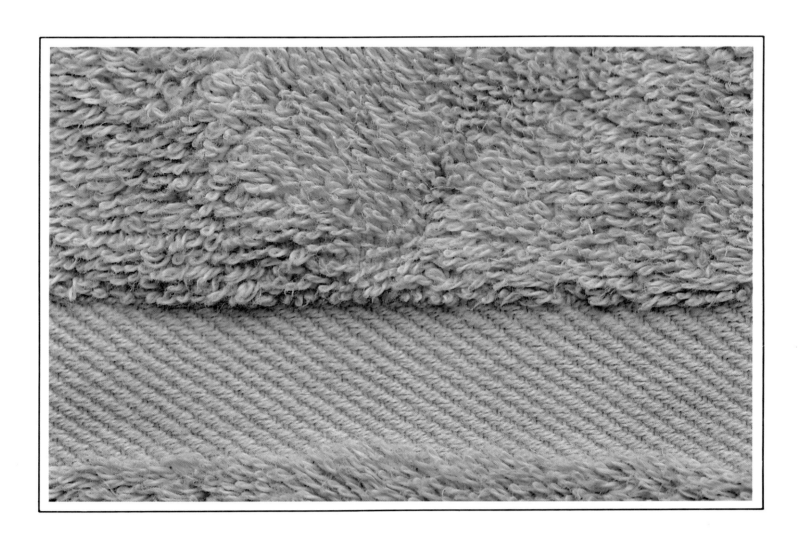

What dries you after your bath?

A towel

What sprays water?

A hose

What do you pull up and down?

A zipper

What can you learn to tie by yourself?

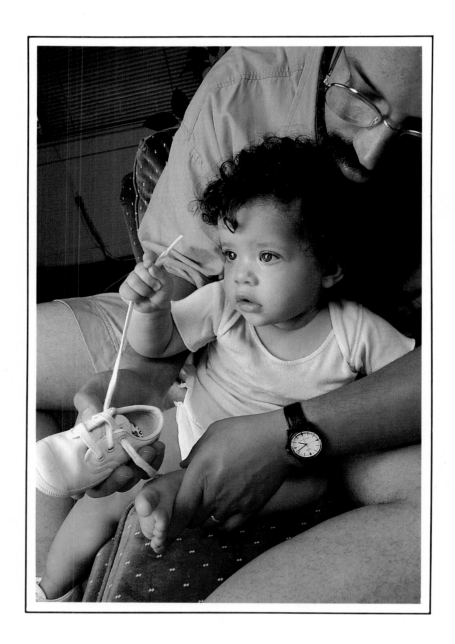

Shoelaces

What do you add each year?

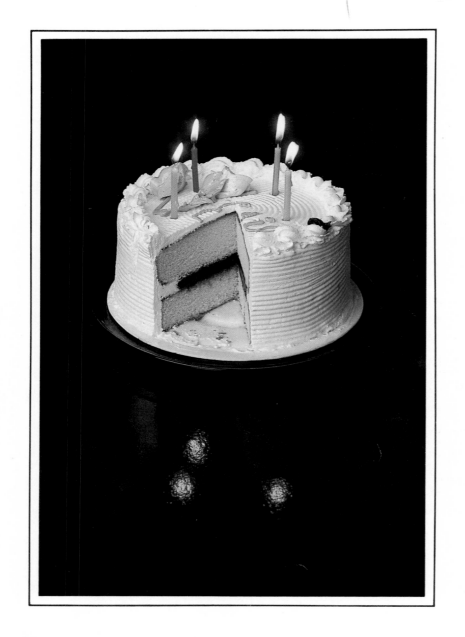

Another birthday candle